P9-DKF-366

3 5674 05442400

CH

AMBER BROWN
IS TICKLED PINK

Paula Danziger's

AMBER BROWN
IS TICKLED PINK

Written by Bruce Coville
and Elizabeth Levy
illustrated by Tony Ross

G. P. PUTNAM'S SONS
AN IMPRINT OF PENGUIN GROUP (USA) INC.

G. P. PUTNAM'S SONS • A division of Penguin Young Readers Group.
Published by The Penguin Group.
Penguin Group (USA) Inc., 375 Hudson Street, New York, NY 10014, U.S.A.
Penguin Group (Canada), 90 Eglinton Avenue East, Suite 700, Toronto,
Ontario M4P 2Y3, Canada (a division of Pearson Penguin Canada Inc.).
Penguin Books Ltd, 80 Strand, London WC2R 0RL, England.
Penguin Ireland, 25 St. Stephen's Green, Dublin 2, Ireland
(a division of Penguin Books Ltd).
Penguin Group (Australia), 250 Camberwell Road, Camberwell, Victoria 3124,
Australia (a division of Pearson Australia Group Pty Ltd).
Penguin Books India Pvt Ltd, 11 Community Centre, Panchsheel Park,
New Delhi—110 017, India.
Penguin Group (NZ), 67 Apollo Drive, Rosedale, Auckland 0632,
New Zealand (a division of Pearson New Zealand Ltd).
Penguin Books (South Africa) (Pty) Ltd, 24 Sturdee Avenue,
Rosebank, Johannesburg 2196, South Africa.
Penguin Books Ltd, Registered Offices: 80 Strand, London
WC2R 0RL, England.

Published simultaneously in Canada. Printed in the United States of America.
Design by Annie Ericsson. Text set in Bembo.
Library of Congress Cataloging-in-Publication Data
Coville, Bruce. Paula Danziger's Amber Brown is tickled pink / written by
Bruce Coville and Elizabeth Levy ; illustrated by Tony Ross.
p. cm. — (Amber Brown chapter books)
Summary: Nine-year-old Amber is nervous and excited about her mother's
wedding to Max, but Amber's father makes things complicated.
[1. Remarriage—Fiction. 2. Weddings—Fiction.] I. Levy, Elizabeth,
1942– II. Ross, Tony, ill. III. Danziger, Paula, 1944–2004. IV. Title.
V. Title: Amber Brown is tickled pink.
PZ7.C8344Pan 2013 [Fic]—dc23 2011039493
ISBN 978-0-399-25656-1
3 5 7 9 10 8 6 4 2

To Paula,

Best friend, best laugh, best first reader, and queen of goofy gifts. You always said we could love each other, but not more than we love you. Well, we both still love you the most, and every day that we worked together on this book, it was as if all three of us were in the room. You would have had so much fun. Thank you for Amber, and thank you for you.

Love,
Bruce and Liz

Chapter One

I, Amber Brown, have to spend a million dollars.

Mrs. Holt just told me so. Actually, everyone in our class has to spend a million dollars.

Too bad it's not real money. . . .

Mrs. Holt says spending a million dollars isn't as easy as you might think. We have to have a lot of facts and figures. And we each have to make a pie chart.

I like eating pies . . . . not charting them.

"When the project is finished, we'll

have a Budget Fair so you can see each other's work," Mrs. Holt tells us.

I think a "Budget Fair" sounds like a place to go on really cheap rides and get half-price cotton candy.

Mrs. Holt starts to make a list of things we have to include:

1. Buy a house
2. Pay for college
3. Give to charity
4. Spend the rest in $25,000 chunks

Mrs. Holt likes lists almost as much as I do, but my lists are more fun. This is math, which is not my best subject. It makes me wish my best friend, Justin Daniels, still lived here. That's nothing new . . . . . everything makes me wish Justin still lived here. But he and his family moved to Alabama last year.

We still talk on the phone and write to

each other, but it's not like having him right across the street.

Bobby Clifford raises his hand. This makes me think he's going to make an armpit fart.

To my surprise, he actually has a question. "What about my car?"

"Put it in your budget . . . . . but remember, I want details. You'll have to research the make and the price." Mrs. Holt raises her arm. "Ready, class? Start your budgets . . . . ." She swooshes her arm down. "NOW!"

Jimmy Russell makes engine noises like he's starting a race car. "Vrooom, vrooom, budget . . . . . vroom! Vroom!"

He is sooooo immature.

Mrs. Holt gives him the teacher look. He stops his engine.

She passes around printouts of real estate listings so we can start our house hunting.

I don't want to look at them. In real life Mom and Max, the guy she's going to marry, just bought a house.

It wasn't so much fun.

I, Amber Brown, am only nine years old, but soon my mother will have her third last name since I've known her . . . which is all my life.

First she was Sarah Brown. Then she and my dad got divorced and she went

back to being Sarah Thompson, which was her name before they got married. Now she's about to become Sarah Turner. It's a good thing her first name isn't Pancake.

I look down at the budget work sheet. Number one is buy a house. We haven't even moved into our new house yet and Mom is already worrying about how much everything costs. She says she feels like she and Max are leaking money. Not to mention worrying about how much the wedding might cost.

Number two is paying for college. During the divorce my mom and dad argued a lot about that. It made my stomach hurt.

So one and two on Mrs. Holt's list make me cranky. Three and four are a lot more fun. I start spending my $25,000 chunks.

1. $25,000 for the Justin Daniels/Amber Brown Travel Fund. That way we can get together whenever we want.

2. The Mom and Max Wedding Fund. In real life, Mom and Max are still figuring out what to do. Max wants a big wedding, Mom wants a small one. I'm with Max on this one. I think we should have an OTT wedding. Kelly Green taught me that phrase. It means "over the top."

I, Amber Brown, am frequently over the top.

3. Speaking of Kelly Green, I would give her $25,000 to get her last name changed. I like Kelly . . . but I'd prefer to be the only kid in class with a colorful name.

What next? I look around the room and get more good ideas.

4. Brandi Colwin gets $25,000 to start an animal beauty parlor. We painted the toenails on her slobbery sheepdog, Darth Vader, once . . . . . one color per nail. Many pets could benefit from this treatment.

5. $25,000 to put on "Pickle Me Silly." That's the musical Brandi and Kelly and I are writing. We were inspired when we saw Brenda . . . . she's my Ambersitter . . . . . in her high school musical. It was so much fun we decided to make one ourselves. So far we have half a song.

6. $25,000 for anti-nose-picking therapy for Fredrich Allen. He could use a

session now. It's such a habit with him, I bet he doesn't even know his index finger is in his left nostril right this minute.

7. I see Hannah Burton staring at herself in her pocket mirror. I bet her charity budget is the "Me, Me, Wonderful Me" Fund. She gets $25,000 for a personality transplant.

Mrs. Holt looks over my shoulder.

"Amber, please remember that you have to present your final project at the Budget Fair. Everyone in class will see it."

I know I have to get serious. I look at my budget notes. I realize I put in something for Mom, but nothing for Dad. That makes me feel bad.

Ever since Mom and Max decided to get married and Dad moved back to town, I, Amber Brown, feel like a division problem.

I don't need a pie chart . . . . . I feel sliced up already.

Chapter Two

"Ta-da!" Dad shouts. "I know who did it!"

I, Amber Brown, am so proud of my father. He has invented a new way to play our favorite game. His version . . . "Clue with Deadly Farts" . . . . . was inspired by the amazingly smelly digestive events of Dylan Marshall, the sixth grader who lives upstairs.

Dylan's sister, Polly, puts down her cards. "All right, who was it?"

"Professor Plum in the library with an

eye-watering bloozer that took the paint off the walls!"

If you're playing with Dylan Marshall, "bloozer" is an important word to know . . . but you never want to be around one.

I always told Mom and Dad I wanted brothers and sisters. When Dad moved into the Marshalls' house, I kind of got them.

Dad lives downstairs and I have my own room. Steve Marshall, who is divorced just like my dad, lives upstairs with his three kids . . . Polly, who is in high school . . . . Dylan, who thinks being gross is his passport to fame . . . and Savannah, who is a third grader.

It's kind of cool. I, Amber Brown, an only child, now spend every other weekend in a house full of kids I actually like . . . . . mostly.

Right now I am really happy to be playing Clue with Deadly Farts. Especially because on Friday, when I left my most-of-the-time house, Mom and Max were fussing about the wedding.

It was starting to scare me. So many things can go wrong when two people get married.

Just look at what happened with Mom and Dad . . . . . or Steve and his wife.

Dylan is so happy with my dad's invention that he's rolling on the floor laughing. "We should make scratch-and-sniff cards to go with this game!" he shouts.

Polly rolls her eyes. "You are soooo disgusting, Dylan!"

But Dad agrees with Dylan. "His idea could make us a million dollars."

"I have a million dollars," I tell them. I explain about my new school project. I don't mention that I forgot to put something for Dad in my first budget.

"That's a good project. I wish your mom had learned about budgeting when she was in school."

I glare at him. He blushes a little. He knows I don't like it when he says bad things about Mom. He's taking dad lessons to try to improve how he behaves with me.

I don't think he's ready to graduate yet.

Unlike Mom and Max, lately Dad has been acting like he doesn't have to worry about money. He just got a new sports car. It's bright red.

Mom calls it his middle-aged-man-starting-over car. I don't know what that means, exactly, but she muttered it in a not very nice way. And she wonders where I get my "Little Miss Amber's Sarcastic Voice."

Dad isn't the only one who could use some lessons in not putting down the other parent.

Dad tells me to pack up so he can take me home.

"Can I come along?" Dylan asks. He loves the new car.

Dad rolls his eyes.

"Oh, right," Dylan says. "I forgot."

One thing I love about the new car is that it only has two seats . . . so there is no room for Dylan. I don't mind Dylan, really . . . . but I'm afraid he might have another digestive event. Since it's too cold to roll down the windows, that could really be deadly. I don't want to end up on a scratch-and-sniff card in our new Clue game.

I tell that to Dad as we're getting in the car. He starts laughing so hard he begins to snort. He gives me a high five. Fortunately, we haven't started driving yet.

I'm going to have to tell Justin about the scratch-and-sniff idea.

As we drive down Chestnut Street, where I live with my mom, I see Max

storm out the front door. He slams it behind him. He looks really, really angry—
something I've never seen before. He gets
in his car and slams that door too.

Max pulls out of the driveway before
Dad and I turn in. I don't think he saw us,
but I know my dad saw him.

I turn to look at Dad. I see the start of
a smug smile.

"Looks like there's trouble in paradise."

This makes me angry. But I'm also

scared. I wonder what happened between Mom and Max.

"Dad, I don't want you to come in." I take a deep breath and then add, "And I don't like it when you say things like that."

His hands get tight on the steering wheel. He stares straight ahead for a minute, then mumbles, "Sorry I upset you, Amber."

I notice he doesn't say he's sorry for what he actually said.

He definitely needs to keep taking those dad lessons.

Now I have to go in the house and see what's going on with Mom.

Sometimes my parents are a lot of work.

Chapter Three

Mom is at the kitchen table. She looks up and tries to pretend that whatever happened wasn't so bad. I can see it was so bad.

"Max and I had our first big fight." She sighs.

My stomach gets tight. "Does this mean you're not getting married?"

I don't know what answer I want for that question. For a long time I wanted my mom and dad to get back together. When Mom first started going out with

Max, I wouldn't even meet him. In fact, I was kind of bratty about it.

But Max turned out to be a really nice guy. He coaches my bowling team, the Pinsters. Also, he laughs at my jokes, even the ones that make Mom groan. My friends all think I'm lucky to have him.

So I do know the answer. I want them to get married.

Mom gets up from the table. She goes to the refrigerator and opens the door. She stares at the shelves, then sighs and closes the door. Turning to me, she says, "No, the wedding isn't off, honey. But with the expense of moving into the new house, I thought it would be better if Max and I went to city hall to get married. We'd take you along, of course, and then go to a nice restaurant for lunch. It's killing me to think of spending so much money on a wedding. Keeping it small would be smarter, but Max hates the idea."

I don't know how to tell Mom, but I'm on Max's side. A tiny wedding is the worst idea I've ever heard.

No Aunt Pam?

No Justin and his family?

Nobody to see the great dress I don't even have yet?

I, Amber Brown, have been studying weddings . . . . . and if I know one thing about them, it's that you really need to have a great party. It's called a reception. Music! Flowers! Food! Dancing! Kelly Green keeps telling me you always do the Chicken Dance at a wedding reception. She says it's so much fun!

Besides all that, I, Amber Brown, have two important jobs at this wedding. I am supposed to be Mom's bridesmaid and also Max's best man . . . . . except Max and I changed that to best child. (Not the best child in the world . . . . . not a chance of that happening!)

I am supposed to give the toast at the party.

At first I wondered if that meant I had to be in the kitchen with some bread. Max explained it means I make a little speech teasing the bride and groom and wishing them good luck.

21

I, Amber Brown, am nervous about this, but I also really want to do it . . . even though I haven't started writing it yet.

All that sure won't happen if we only go to city hall.

And another thing . . . . . Mom told me I could invite Kelly Green and Brandi Colwin to the wedding. I already did it. What if now I have to tell them they can't come?

The more I think about this, the rottener it gets.

"Mom, that is the worst idea that you have ever come up with. It's worse than . . . . . worse than . . . . . worse than liver pancakes with broccoli syrup!"

I get a little smile from Mom. It doesn't last long, but at least she doesn't look like she's going to cry anymore.

I go to the refrigerator and get out some ice cream. It doesn't solve all problems, but it works for Mom and me sometimes.

She gives me another little smile. Then she sighs.

The phone rings.

"See who that is, would you, honey?" She sighs again.

I am getting tired of these sighs. There are two sighs to everything, and Mom has just passed her limit.

I run to the phone. It's Max! He sounds serious. "Hi, Amber, can I talk to your mom, please?"

I hold out the phone and whisper, "It's him!"

Mom shakes her head. I'm worried that she'll say sigh-onara. That's Japanese for "good-bye." We learned it in Mr. Cohen's third-grade class. I don't want her to say good-bye to Max now.

"Mom, you have to talk to him."

She sighs again. "I know. I'll take it in my room."

As she gets up, I say to Max, "Mom will be on in just a minute."

"Is she upset?"

"Duh!"

He sighs. This is like an epidemic.

Mom's voice breaks in. "I've got it, Amber. You can hang up now."

I don't think I can get away with listening in. So I hang up and go to my room.

Mom and Max talk for a long time. I know because I keep one eye on the light on the phone that shows it's being used and the other on my pig-taking-a-bubble-bath alarm clock. Aunt Pam gave me the piggy . . . . it's also a bank. Looking at it now makes me wish I really had that million dollars from Mrs. Holt's class. Then I could make this problem go away.

I pick up my plastic mermaid. She has blond hair, a blue plastic body and tail, and a jewel in her stomach. When you press the jewel, weird music comes out.

I tried to win her in a burping contest last fall. I lost to Gregory Gifford. He burped ninety-two times in a row. Then he burped the alphabet for a victory lap.

I didn't have a chance.

I was sooooo disappointed about not getting the mermaid. Mom told Max about it and he searched and searched and finally found one for me. And that was before I even met him. That's the kind of guy he is.

I press the jewel and try to sing along. But then I sigh. This is definitely an epidemic.

Finally the light on the phone goes out. I wait for Mom to come talk to me, but she doesn't. I wait as long as I can. According to the piggy, it's two minutes.

When I can't stand it anymore, I go knock on Mom's door.

When she opens her door, she's smiling. "I was just coming to talk to you, sweetie. It's all going to be okay. Max has agreed to have a small wedding with no reception. We'll have a few more people . . . . . just family. Max's parents and Aunt Pam will probably fly in. But that's it. Max isn't happy about it, but he admits that all the places we looked at for the reception were way too expensive. It's just not a good time to spend so much money."

"Will I still get to be the best child?"

"Oh, honey, you're always the best child to me."

I, Amber Brown, know that Mom means that. But if I was really the best child, I would find a way for us to have a great party.

I need to talk to Justin.

Chapter Four

Mom and I have a deal. For every five papers I bring home that have an A, I can make a call to Justin.

I'm not crazy about this deal. I would rather be able to call Justin every night. But I have to admit my grades have gotten better since it started. Now I cash in one of my "Make a call to Justin" cards.

Mrs. Daniels answers the phone. "Hello, Amber. This is a nice surprise!" She sounds happy to hear my voice.

We talk for a little bit, then she says, "I

can't wait to come up and see you this spring for the wedding."

I wonder what she's going to think when she finds out there is not going to be a wedding party after all. I decide to let Mom deal with that.

"Uh-oh. The baby is starting to cry. I'll get Justin. I know who you really want to talk to anyway."

Justin gets on the phone.

"Justin, we have a problem!"

"You think you've got a problem? Try having a new baby in the house."

I feel bad. I was so upset about the wedding that I forgot I should ask about the baby first.

"Is she still a barfburger?" That was what Justin called her the first week after she was born.

He doesn't answer right away. "Promise not to tell anyone?"

"I promise. Not to tell what?"

"I love having her in my lap. She mostly just sleeps and eats right now, but sometimes she grabs my finger and holds on tight. I didn't like it much when Danny was born, but I was a little kid then. This is different."

I have never heard Justin sound like this before. He keeps changing while I am not looking.

"So what's the problem?" he asks.

"Mom has decided to call off the big party and have a tiny wedding at city hall instead."

"That's okay. I don't like big parties anyway."

"You don't understand. If we don't have a big wedding, even you won't be invited. I may not see you for a billion years. We won't get to do the Chicken Dance!"

"Is that where you lay an egg?"

"Yuk! Yuk!"

"Didn't you mean 'Yolk! Yolk!'"

I snort. "Stop, you're cracking me up!"

It feels good to laugh. But it doesn't solve the party problem. Justin just keeps telling me he's sure it will all work out.

He has always had a hard time talking

about problems. I can tell he wants to change the subject.

He does. "How's our chewing gum ball?"

When Justin and I were little kids, we started making a ball from our ABC . . .

"Already Been Chewed" . . . gum. It's the kind of thing our parents thought we'd get tired of doing, but we didn't.

I got custody of it when he moved. He still sends gum support . . . . his used chewing gum. He sticks the gum in a wet paper towel and then puts plastic wrap around it. When a letter comes, I always know if there's gum support in it because the envelope is lumpy.

Sometimes it's also slightly soggy.

I keep the ball in my closet because my mother thinks it's gross and doesn't want to see it.

I'm going to have to be careful that there's no "Let's throw out the chewing gum ball" campaign when we move to the new house.

I tell Justin that the ball is growing nicely, but he's behind on his gum support.

After Justin and I say good-bye, I'm in a better mood . . . but not for long. I really, really miss him.

And I really, really, really want him at the wedding.

Chapter
Five

"Okay, Amber, what's wrong?" Brandi asks.

She and Kelly have cornered me on the playground, or, as we like to call it, the hang-around-and-talk ground.

"What do you mean?" I try to sound as if I have no idea what she's talking about.

Kelly gives me a look. "Oh, come on, Amber. Today's the day Fredrich's father is coming to talk to us."

Every other Monday, Mrs. Holt invites a parent to visit and tell us about their lives. Some people have much more interesting lives than other people do.

"What's Fredrich's father got to do with anything?"

Brandi rolls her eyes. "Normally you would have made at least three nose-picking jokes by now. You haven't even made one. Clearly something is bugging you."

Actually, I had wondered if nose-picking ran in the Allen family. But Kelly and Brandi are right. I haven't even made that easy joke about noses running. I am too upset about the wedding.

Last night it was easy to say to myself that I, Amber Brown, will save the day. But the truth is I don't have a clue about what to do.

"Well?" Brandi waits for an answer.

I sigh. Apparently the sighing epidemic lasts for more than twenty-four hours. I

don't want to tell them what's going on. But I know that's what friends do . . . . . tell each other when something is wrong.

I take a deep breath . . . . . I try not to sigh. . . . "It's Mom and Max."

"They're not calling the wedding off, are they?" Kelly asks.

"No, no. But they want to make it a lot smaller."

"Like downsizing?" Brandi sounds worried.

Brandi's father has been out of work for the last two months because his company let people go to save money. . . . . . They called it downsizing.

None of us had heard that word before. Now we hate it.

"Real small," I answer, "unless I can figure something out. Mom says a big wedding is too expensive, but I know Max still really, really wants one. I do too.

I wish our million-dollar project was real. I need a lot of money fast."

"You could get a job," Brandi suggests.

"Like what?"

Kelly giggles. "You could be a glitter consultant."

"I could open a peanut butter and M&M sandwich shop." I know we are being silly, but it's making me feel better.

Before we can think of more ways for me to make money, Mrs. Holt lines us up. "Recess is over. It's time to meet Fredrich's father."

"I wonder if he has a skunk farm," Brandi says. "Remember when Fredrich's brother put that skunk in the school at the beginning of the year?"

Now I giggle. "That was the stinkiest school day ever. It was a good day to keep boogers IN your nose . . . so you couldn't smell anything!"

Kelly grins. "She's back!!!!"

Fredrich's dad is tall and kind of good-looking. Instead of a white shirt and tie like some dads have worn, he's wearing jeans and a sweatshirt. The sweatshirt says CAMP SUKKATUKKET in big blue letters.

Mr. Allen turns out to be more interesting than I expected. He owns and runs a summer camp, which is on Sukkatukket Pond. I've never heard of it before, but I'm already thinking of funny camp songs using that name.

Bobby Clifford waves his hand. "Does that mean you only work in the summer?"

Mr. Allen laughs. "Not hardly. Taking care of a place like Camp Sukkatukket is a year-round job. There's always something that needs repairing or fixing."

While his dad is talking, Fredrich passes out brochures. I check mine to make sure it is booger-free before I open it.

The place looks pretty nice. It's on a pond. Well, actually, it isn't ON the pond because then it would be underwater, or at least heading that way.

I think it is very strange the way people use words sometimes.

"Fredrich and I work on the camp every weekend," Mr. Allen says. "It's vacant in the winter, of course, but sometimes during spring and fall we rent it out for special events."

There are two things I like about Mr. Allen.

Number one: He hasn't picked his nose even once.

Number two: He's just given me a great idea. And this one could work!

Chapter
Six

I, Amber Brown, am so happy. I just got
the last stamp on my Frequent Dumpling
Card. That means that the next time we
go to Charlie Woo's Happy Panda Chinese
Restaurant, I get my dumplings free.

On the Saturdays I'm not with Dad,
Mom, Max, and I like to have dim sum at
Happy Panda. It's my favorite meal. You
don't even have to order. They just keep
wheeling dumplings around. You choose
as many as you want . . . . . and there are
so many different kinds!

Mom is using her chopsticks to pick up
a shrimp dumpling.

Max and I hate chopsticks, so we use

forks. Well, mostly. Sometimes I use my fingers. So does Max . . . . but only when Mom's not looking.

Mom puts down her chopsticks. "What shall we do this afternoon?"

"It's a beautiful day," Max says. "Let's take a drive."

I can't believe how lucky I am. This is the perfect opening. "Can I choose where we go? Oh please, oh please, oh please!"

I, Amber Brown, am very good at pleading.

It helps that Mom and Max are still feeling guilty because I have been so upset about their fight and about the tiny wedding.

I see Max smiling. I can tell he is about to say yes when Mom stops him.

"Max, you can't tell Amber something like that without setting a limit. Trust me on this. Next thing you know, she'll have us driving to Alabama to see Justin."

"I hadn't thought of that. What a great idea!"

"See what I mean?"

Max is laughing. "Okay, Amber . . . . . anyplace you want to go within . . . . . hmmmmm, within forty miles."

That worries me because I'm not sure how far it is to Sukkatukket Pond.

"So where are we going?" Mom wants to know.

"You'll see. I'm going to program it into Max's GPS."

Mom smiles. "Little Miss Mystery."

That's a new name for me. I like it.

We go to the car. "All right," I say, "you two stay out here while I program Adrianne."

Max named his GPS Adrianne after his aunt because she's always telling him where to go.

"Okay," Mom says. "Only don't take too long. It's a beautiful day, but it's pretty chilly."

In the car I pull the brochure out of my coat pocket. It does take me a long time to punch in Sukkatukket Pond. But I'm relieved to find out that it's only twenty-one miles away.

"Ready!" I shout.

I ask Mom to sit in the backseat since I am in control. Well, me and Adrianne.

Max turns around to Mom. "Relax and enjoy the ride, honey. And don't worry. Wherever Adrianne takes us, she can get us home."

It really is a beautiful day. The sky is clear, and the sun sparkles on the patches of snow still left on the ground. We pass some farms. Then Adrianne tells us to turn onto a narrow road that goes through a forest.

Max starts singing, "And did we ever return, no, we never returned!"

"Amber, are you sure you know where we're going?" Mom sounds nervous.

"Sure," I say . . . though I am starting to wonder myself.

I wonder even more when we turn onto a bumpy dirt road.

Finally Adrianne chirps. "Destination three hundred yards ahead on the right."

"Whew," Max says. "That's a relief."

Mom reads the sign: WELCOME TO CAMP SUKKATUKKET. "Amber, is this really where you wanted us to go?"

"Yep. It belongs to one of my friends from school. His dad came to tell us about it, and I've been wanting to see it ever since."

The part about friends is kind of a white lie . . . . . Fredrich and I aren't really friends . . . . . I've seen him knuckle-deep in his nose too many times for that. But at least we know each other.

46

In February, Camp Sukkatukket doesn't look anywhere near as good as it does in the brochure. The driveway is muddy and rutty. Just inside the gate is a small building with a sagging roof and boarded-up windows. The sign says CHECK IN HERE . . . . . but it looks more like a place to check out.

I start to wonder if my great idea is really so great.

Mom is starting to look nervous. "I don't think we should go any farther. Aren't we trespassing?"

"Fredrich's dad said they are up here every weekend," I tell her. "I want to say hi to Fredrich."

Another little white lie.

We drive on, going slow because of the mud and ruts. The trees are all bare, though I suppose that's not their fault. We come to the parking lot. It's empty except

for an SUV and two big Dumpsters. Not pretty.

Then we see the pond and it *is* pretty. The sun is sparkling on the water.

I like sparkles. I feel better. We hear hammering and look toward the sounds. Fredrich and his dad are working on the cabin porch.

"We'd better let them know we're here," Mom says.

I get a little nervous about my great plan. What's Fredrich going to do when he sees me?

I find out. When Fredrich spots us, he drops his hammer and starts hopping on one foot.

I guess I know where the hammer landed.

Fredrich's father waves to us and comes down the cabin steps.

Max waves back. "Hi. We were out for

a drive and Amber wanted us to come see your camp."

"I remember you, Amber," says Mr. Allen. "You're in Fredrich's class."

Fredrich's dad smiles, but Fredrich is staring at me with his mouth open.

"Hi, Fredrich," I say. "Nice to see you."

Another little white lie.

Fredrich comes off the porch and stands next to his dad.

"Let me show you around," Mr. Allen says. "The place is a little muddy right now, but it will look a lot better come spring."

We walk along a path with cabins on each side. He takes us into one. It's nicer on the inside than it looks from the outside.

Mom smiles. "This is cozy."

I take this as a good sign.

Next we walk to a big wooden building. "This is Sukkatukket Lodge," Mr. Allen says proudly. "It's our main building. The dining hall is here, and also our big function room. We call it the Grand Salon. It has a stage, and in summer we have dances every Wednesday and Saturday night. And, of course, we're famous for the sunset view from the Sukkatukket Verandah."

He takes us to the verandah . . . . . I'd call it a porch . . . . . a really big porch. It is wider than our living room and stretches all the way across the front of the lodge.

Mom looks out at the pond. "This is lovely."

Luckily she isn't looking at Fredrich. He has his finger in his nose. No surprise to me. I expected it earlier.

His dad swats his arm and says in a low voice, "Do you want me to make you start wearing gloves again?"

Fredrich blushes and pulls his hand away from his nose. He puts his hand in his pocket.

I try to pretend that I didn't hear his dad, but I can tell Fredrich knows I did.

Normally I would wonder if he had a booger in his pocket.

Today, I just feel a little sorry for him.

Chapter Seven

Mom and Max are holding hands. They are staring out at the pond. Mom lays her head on Max's shoulder. It's so perfect that I feel like this is the moment.

I turn to Fredrich's father and blurt, "Do you ever have weddings here?"

"AMBER!" Mom says.

"Sure we do," Mr. Allen says. "Mostly in the off-season. Are you two getting married?"

"Yes," Max tells him. "Later this spring."

Mr. Allen smiles. "And you're still looking for a place?"

I can tell he thinks my idea is as good as
I do.

I hold my breath, hoping that Mom
doesn't say, "No, we're all set. We're going
to city hall."

Mom and Max look at each other but
don't say anything.

Mr. Allen jumps in. "Since Amber and
Fredrich are in the same class, I can give

you the friends and family discount. And if the wedding is before June first, we can do even better. I think you'll be surprised at the price. Why don't you come inside and we can talk?"

"Sure." Max answers before Mom can say anything.

She looks a little flummoxed. But she follows them.

I cross my fingers on both hands. Make it work, I think, make it work!

Then I realize I'm alone on the porch with Fredrich. I don't think I've ever been alone with him before.

"It would be nice if they get married here," he says.

"It's pretty." I try to think of something else to say, but I'm surprised to find that I, Amber Brown, am out of words.

"Do you want to walk down to the pond?" Fredrich asks.

"Will there be skunks?"

"They don't usually come out in the daytime."

I glance through the window. I can see Mom and Max talking to Mr. Allen.

"Don't worry, we've got time. Once Dad gets started, it will take them a while to get away from him. He's a really good salesman."

I hope he's a super-salesman. I look at the pond again. "Okay, let's go."

I don't really want to spend that much time alone with Fredrich, but I need to give his dad lots of time to work on Mom and Max.

We go by a bonfire pit.

"We have the best campfires," Fredrich says. "Lots of sing-alongs. Dad knows tons of professional musicians. They love to come here in the summer."

Fredrich's life is more interesting than I had realized. "How long have you had this place?"

"My grandfather started the camp. I really love it here. My whole family does. That's why my brother Marvin was so upset when Dad banned him from camp until June."

"Why did he do that?"

"Because this is where Marvin got the skunk that he put in the school. I'm glad I was smart enough not to help him with that one or I'd be at home today too. My dad is pretty tough."

Fredrich smiles. It surprises me. He doesn't smile that often in school.

This is the longest conversation Fredrich and I have ever had.

In fact, it's the only conversation we've ever had.

The pond has a nice sandy beach. Fredrich shows me the boathouse . . . . it's full of canoes and kayaks.

We go to the lifeguard tower. "Can I climb it?"

"Sure!"

I go to the top. I love it up there. It's got a great view!

I turn around and see Mom and Max back on the porch.

I wave to them and climb down. "Let's go," I say to Fredrich. "I want to find out what's happening."

As we get closer, I see that Max is grinning. Mom isn't exactly grinning, but she doesn't look unhappy either.

"Come on, Fredrich," Mr. Allen says. "We need to get to back to work. You folks stay here as long as you want. Come say good-bye before you leave."

I grin at them. "Soooooooooo?"

Max grins too. "It's really a great price."

Mom makes a face.

"Come on, Sarah. This would actually cost less than we planned on before we even started looking. It's the price tag we were after but couldn't find in town. It wouldn't be formal, it wouldn't be fancy, but it would be a load of fun."

Wow! This idea is even better than I thought!

"Oh, I don't know," Mom says. "City hall would be so easy."

The time has come for the best, most powerful begging I have ever done.

I drop to my knees and fold my hands in front of me. "Oh please!" I cry. "Oh please, oh please, oh please, oh purple please, oh glorious please, oh please like I've never asked for anything before. Let's have the wedding here with all our friends!"

A smile twitches at the corner of Mom's mouth.

Suddenly Max drops down beside me. He stretches his arms toward Mom. "Oh please!" he cries. "Oh please, my beloved, my darling, my jelly bean!"

He's good at this!

Mom starts to laugh.

"Oh please, queen of all mothers!" I cry. "Oh please, mother of the best child!"

Max spreads his arms wide. "Oh please, my glorious bride-to-be. With but one word you can make our day."

"Our week!" I spread my arms wide too.

"Our year!" Max cries.

"All right, all right!" Mom gasps. "Let's have the wedding here. Just stop begging. My stomach hurts."

Victory!

Max and I hop up and share a high five.

A lot of people say the way to a man's heart is through his stomach.

Fortunately for me and Max, one way to Mom's heart is through her funny bone.

Chapter Eight

"How about this one?" Aunt Pam says. "It's not pink."

"No, it's outer-space green," I say.

The dress is iridescent, which means shiny. And yes, I like shiny, but this one looks like an alien ate something that didn't agree with it.

I give Aunt Pam my "I can't believe you expect me to wear this dress" face. It's a face I've been making all day. Aunt Pam is getting exasperated. Mom is getting exasperated. The saleswoman is getting

exasperated . . . . . . and we've been to six
stores before we even got to her.

I, Amber Brown, am exasperated too. I
am also disgruntled, peeved, and put out.
I have nothing to wear. I don't mean that
I'm naked. But now that we are having
the wedding, I must, must, MUST have
THE dress!

It's not going to be alien green.

It's also not going to be pink. Not that there's anything wrong with pink. I like pink. I have a pink knapsack. But I told Aunt Pam and Mom when this long day began that I don't think the best child should look like cotton candy.

I'm not going to wear a little tuxedo suit either. That was Aunt Pam's idea.

Aunt Pam is here because now that the wedding is big again, or at least medium big, she decided to fly in from California to help with the preparations. She used her frequent-flyer miles. Aunt Pam loves frequent-flyer miles as much as I love my Frequent Dumpling Card.

I, Amber Brown, think there should be Frequent Cards for everything.

Mom already has her dress. She got it two months ago when she was visiting Aunt Pam.

For her wedding with Dad, Mom wore a white satin dress with a long train. I don't mean that it had a whistle and a caboose, just that it trailed along on the floor about ten feet behind her. Dad was in a tuxedo. The two of them looked a little like those couples you see on top of wedding cakes.

I know this because their wedding picture used to hang on their bedroom wall.

Now the picture is in my closet, next to the chewing gum ball.

The dress Mom's going to wear to marry Max isn't really that fancy. But it is really, really pretty. The only bad thing is that it's a color Mom and Aunt Pam call "ochre."

I, Amber Brown, know a lot about names of colors and ochre is the worst one I've ever heard. It's sounds like that slimy green vegetable, okra. But it's not.

Mom's dress is kind of caramel-colored. I think caramel is what they should call it.

I try on three more dresses and hate them all. They should have been labeled UGLY, UGLIER, and UGLIEST.

"Amber," Aunt Pam says, "if you're not careful, you'll end up going to the wedding in a burlap sack."

"It'll be better than this." I hand a turquoise monstrosity back to the clerk.

"That's it," Mom says. "It's time to call it a day. We've got plenty of other things to worry about."

The clerk looks relieved.

When we get to the car, Aunt Pam offers to drive. "You've got too much on your mind, Sarah."

"Okay, but hurry. Max is coming over so we can finalize the guest list. The problem is, he has more cousins than Amber has mismatched socks. There's no way we can invite all of them."

I thought I liked lists, but this guest list is driving us all crazy. Max keeps trying to put people on. Mom keeps trying to take people off.

It's a trying situation.

"We should make a set of Max's cousins trading cards," I say.

Aunt Pam laughs. "Good idea! Your mom and Max can trade cards back and forth until there's a list they agree on. Oh, and we could save them to use as favors!"

Mom groans. "Favors! I forgot about favors. Remind me to put that on the THINGS WE HAVE TO DO FOR THIS DARN WEDDING list."

I tell her that phrase is a sign of a bad attitude. I like saying this because she is always bothering me about my attitude.

Mom sighs. "You're right. Please don't

tell Max I said it. I just forgot about the favors."

"Okay, but I'm confused. Are we supposed to do favors for people, like walking their dogs or mowing their lawns? What does that have to do with the wedding?"

Aunt Pam laughs. "It's fun to give a little gift to everybody who comes to the wedding, something to remember it by. That's what people call a favor. I was thinking, Amber, that you and your friends could make the favors. They could have glitter."

"Glitterific!"

Mom doesn't even roll her eyes. She is looking a little cross-eyed. It's not a good look for a bride.

We pull into the driveway.

Max is already there waiting for us. "What took you so long? Did you get a dress, Amber?"

"Don't ask," I say.

Max raises his eyebrows, but puts his hands over his mouth.

We go inside.

Max uncovers his mouth and says, "I've got good news. I think we've solved the music problem."

I know music is a problem because Mom and Max have been complaining that every band and DJ they've checked out is too expensive.

"Really?" Mom sounds suspicious.

"Really! Herman and Rose offered to do the music as a wedding gift."

"Who are Herman and Rose?" Aunt Pam and I ask together.

"A couple of my second cousins. I just love them. You will too."

"I get the Herman and Rose card!" I whisper to Aunt Pam.

"They're musicians," Max says. "They

perform at Renaissance fairs . . . . . you know, the ones with jousting and everything. They're great!"

"Justin and me jousting . . . he'll love it," I say.

Aunt Pam scowls at me. "No jousting at the wedding!"

Mom is looking a little skeptical. "You're not telling me that you want our guests to come to the wedding in costume, are you?"

"Of course not. Well, Herman and Rose will be in costume. I don't think they own any normal clothes. But no one else has to dress that way."

"It's not very traditional," Mom says.

"Are you kidding? The music is five hundred years old. It's super-traditional! Besides, it will make our wedding unique . . . like us!"

"I don't know." Mom hesitates.

"At least meet them and hear their music. They invited us over tonight. They want to play for us."

"Wagons ho!" Aunt Pam sings out. "We're off to see Rose and Herman!"

"Field trip!" I shout.

Mom sighs. She can tell when she's beat.

Chapter Nine

As we get in the car, Aunt Pam sings, "She's his Rose and Herman's her man!"

Max joins in.

I don't even know the song Aunt Pam is singing, but it has a pun in it, and that makes me happy. It's giving me a good feeling about Herman and Rose. I just hope I'm right.

As Max and Aunt Pam start a second verse, Mom leans back and moans, "What did I do to deserve this?"

"You fell in love with this adorable man," Aunt Pam says.

I, Amber Brown, am feeling very good. Here I am in the car with three of the four people I love most, laughing and singing and making jokes, on our way to cross off one more item on Mom's THINGS WE HAVE TO DO FOR THIS DARN WEDDING list.

After about twenty minutes we come to a town with a sign that says

GEORGE WASHINGTON
HEADQUARTERED
HERE

Ten minutes later we come to the same sign.

"Didn't we see that sign two towns ago?" Aunt Pam asks.

"George Washington headquartered all over New Jersey in 1776," I tell her. "He was being chased by the British, but then he pulled off a brilliant sneak attack. Mrs. Holt taught us that."

I like knowing this. I am proud of my state. I think all kids should be proud of their state.

"Here we are!" Max pulls into the driveway of a big, very old-fashioned house.

"Is this what homes looked like in the Renaissance?" I ask.

"No, Amber, this is a Victorian," Mom explains. "They came later."

"I love these old Victorians," Aunt Pam says. "We don't have many in Southern California."

As we get out of the car, the front door of the house opens. Out step two very odd-looking people. Well, their clothes are kind of odd. The people just look extremely happy. They must be Herman and Rose.

"Maxila!" Herman runs down the front steps and throws his arms around Max.

Rose is right behind him. "And which of you lovely ladies is Sarah?"

Aunt Pam points to Mom and moves a step back. She barely makes it before Rose sweeps Mom into a big hug.

Rose is little and round. If you put her in a red suit, she would make a perfect Mrs. Santa.

Herman couldn't be Santa, though, because he is tall and skinny. He does have a beard, but it's short and dark brown.

Rose turns to me. "And you must be Amber . . . . . Amber Brown. Such a colorful name . . . . twice as many colors as mine! Max tells me you're colorful enough to deserve it."

I like her already.

We go inside. Musical instruments are hanging on every wall. They also cover one of the tables, the couch, and all of the chairs. I don't even know the names of most of them.

The one I do know is the harp. It's standing in a corner all its own. It's taller than I am, and just seeing it makes me wish I could play it.

"Sit right down and I'll bring you some hot chocolate," says Rose. She looks around the room and sees that there is an instrument on every place that we could possibly sit. She snatches something that looks like a guitar from one of the chairs. Herman picks up two other instruments and moves them to the table.

While they are doing this, I have time to look at them more carefully. Rose's face is round and merry. She has a braid coiled at each side of her head. Her dress is dark green velvet and down to the floor. The sleeves have white lace from the elbows to the wrists.

Herman is wearing a black velvet cap. He has soft leather boots that reach almost to his knees. His leather vest has silver buttons. Under it is a white shirt with puffy sleeves.

"Before we play, let us get you that hot chocolate," Rose says. She and Herman head for the kitchen.

Aunt Pam is smiling. "They're delightful!"

"Do they dress like that all the time?" I whisper to Max.

"I've never seen them in modern clothes. But this is dressier than usual. I think they did it for us, Sarah." He takes Mom's hand.

She smiles but looks a little uncertain.

"Here we go!" Rose sings. She is carrying a silver tray with six mugs of hot chocolate on it. Herman is right behind her with another tray. This one is filled with cookies. I am liking these two more and more.

Herman looks at Mom. "I don't know if you've heard any of our music, Sarah, so we thought we'd play you some of the songs we've done at other weddings."

Rose sits down at the harp. Herman picks up a flute and stands near her. They nod to each other and start to play. At first the music sounds odd to me, but after a few minutes it starts to feel almost magical, as if it's casting a spell.

I look at Mom. She has a soft smile on

her face. I can tell the music is getting to her too.

Rose stands up. "We thought that song would be right for the ceremony."

Mom nods. "It's perfect."

"Who's performing the service?" Rose asks. "We can work out the details with them."

"We haven't chosen anyone yet," Max tells her.

"Rose can do it," Herman says. "She's been performing marriages for years."

"We've been thinking of writing our own vows," Mom tells them. She sounds a little shy about it. I realize this must be important. Mom's been keeping it private . . . . . . it's not even on her To Do list.

It reminds me that I need to get to work on my toast . . . . the top item on my own To Do list.

Rose beams at Mom. "That's the kind of wedding I like best."

"Good," Herman says. "That settles that! Now let's talk about the music for the party afterward. Better yet, let's play some."

He hands Rose a tambourine. Then he picks up a weird instrument that looks like a chunky violin with a crank on its bottom. "This is a hurdy-gurdy. They've been around for almost a thousand years. I built this one myself. It's one of my favorite instruments. You'll want to dance when you hear this tune."

He sits and plops it into his lap, then starts cranking and plucking. Rose bangs her tambourine. The song is so fast and lively, it makes my feet want to move. Max starts to clap along. Soon we are all clapping.

"Dance!" Herman cries.

Rose hands me the tambourine. While I start to bang and shake it, she grabs Max by the hand. She pulls him up and they dance. A minute later Mom and Aunt Pam are dancing. Me too. Now everyone except Herman is whirling around the room. He's busy cranking the hurdy-gurdy.

The song ends. Everyone is laughing and out of breath.

Maybe I can get Herman to help us with the music for "Pickle Me Silly."

Mom has a big grin on her face. "Herman and Rose, thank you for this. It will be a joy to have you play at our wedding."

Rose gives her a hug. "Sarahila, you're going to make the most beautiful bride."

Then she hugs me. The soft velvet of her dress feels good. She stands back. "Amberila," she says, pinching me on the cheek.

Normally I try to avoid cheek pinchers. Somehow from Rose I don't mind. I look at Max. He winks at me.

As we head for the car, Herman hands Mom a CD. "Listen to this and pick some of your favorite songs. We'll make sure to play them at the wedding."

We get in the car. "Maxila? Sarahila? Amberila?" I ask Max.

"It just means she loves us."

He sounds so happy.

As we drive home, we listen to the CD. We laugh and sing along. When we get home, Max opens the car door for me. "Amberila," he says, making a little bow.

"Let's not make that name a habit," I tell him. But I'm laughing.

We go into the house. The phone is ringing.

"I'll get it." Mom picks up the phone.

The smile leaves her face.

She hands the phone to me. "It's your dad." She nods to Max. The two of them and Aunt Pam go into the kitchen.

"Hi, Daddy!"

"How's my little girl? I've been trying to call. What have you been up to?"

"Oh, nothing much, just some errands." I feel like it would be mean to say what we were really doing.

I wonder if he can tell that I'm kind of fibbing. But he's too excited to notice.

"Listen, honey, I'm planning a big surprise for three weekends from now. That's supposed to be our weekend anyway, but I want to make sure that your mom isn't going to ask us to change our plans."

I can tell he's trying to be nice about it. He almost succeeds.

"What are we going to do?"

"Now that, my little pookanilly, is going to be the surprise."

"Dad!" I say.

"Amber!" he says.

We talk for a while longer. When it's time to say good-bye, we have a kissing contest. To do this, we both make kissy sounds into the phone as fast as we can for as long as we can. The one who gets in the most kisses before we say good-bye wins.

"I give up," he says after about a minute. "My lips hurt!"

I don't tell him that my lips hurt too. I was not going to stop until I won.

I hang up and turn around. Mom and Max are standing in the doorway, watching me.

Suddenly I feel weird.

I love my dad.

I love Mom and Max.

I just don't love having to think about all of them at the same time.

I, Amber Brown, realize that for the first time in my life something huge is happening and Dad isn't even a tiny part of it.

He can't be and that makes me sad.

Sometimes happy and sad come so close together in my life that I can't keep track of how I'm feeling.

Chapter Ten

"I have great news." I am in the lunch-room with Brandi and Kelly. "The wedding party is on and you're still invited."

"Yay!" Brandi cheers.

Then I tell them about Herman and Rose.

Kelly is excited. "They sound totally cool!"

"And we're going to have it at Camp Sukkatukket."

I should have quit while I was ahead.

"Bulletin! Bulletin! Bulletin!" Brandi

wants to be a newscaster when she grows up and she believes in getting an early start.

Before I can stop her, she announces to the entire lunchroom that my mother is getting married at Camp Sukkatukket.

The tables around us go quiet.

Jimmy Russell breaks the silence. This is no surprise. "Wow!" he shouts. "Are you going to serve boogers on toast for appetizers?"

He is sitting at an all-boys table next to us.

Bobby Clifford slaps Fredrich on the back. "At last you can get rid of all those boogers you've got in the freezer."

"You boys are disgusting." Hannah Burton curls her lip. Then she turns to me and puts on her sympathetic face.

I know this is a dangerous sign.

"I'm so sorry to hear this, Amber. I suppose it was the only place you could afford.

I do hope you put money in the budget for
skunk control and stink removal."

I wonder if there is a skunk in Hannah's family tree. She is definitely a little
stinker . . . . . make that an enormous
stinker.

Trying to ignore her, I tell Brandi and
Kelly that the three of us are in charge of
making favors for the reception.

"How about Eau du Skunk?" Kelly
asks. "We can put it in little perfume
bottles."

"And we can write out the guests'
names in glitter boogers," Brandi suggests.

Usually I like booger jokes. I've made lots of them about Fredrich the nose picker. But now I see him slump down as though he wants to slip under the table.

I think about his father swatting his hand. I also remember how proud he was when he took me around the camp.

Turning to Brandi, I say, "Bulletin. Bulletin. Bulletin. Camp Sukkatukket is really a beautiful place. Fredrich took me on a tour. It's got a pretty, pretty pond, and when you stand on the lodge porch you can see the sunset."

I say this too loudly. I know I am too loud because the boys hear me.

"Oooh!" Jimmy Russell says. "Fredrich and Amber, sitting on the porch, love so hot it starts to scorch!"

Now I'm beginning to feel like *I* want to go under the table. Except I don't want to meet Fredrich there.

Hannah Burton looks as happy as I've

ever seen her. Watching other people, particularly me, get embarrassed is Hannah heaven.

"Amber, I know your standards are low, but really . . ."

Hannah doesn't finish the sentence. She doesn't need to. Her smile says it all.

Kelly and Brandi are also looking like they want to slip under the table.

"I'm sorry I announced that bulletin," Brandi whispers to me.

I'm sorry I ever told Brandi and Kelly about the camp. Except they had to know sooner or later if they were going to come to the wedding.

"It's not really your fault," I whisper back.

"I made the joke about the skunk perfume," Kelly says.

"The glitter boogers were mine," Brandi admits.

"ENOUGH! No more booger jokes

about this wedding. And the camp is beautiful. And . . ." I pause. "And Fredrich is nice."

Hannah opens her mouth. She makes that smug face she has when she's about to say something really mean.

I shoot her my best "Don't you dare" look, which is something I learned from Mom.

It works. Hannah shuts her mouth.

I, Amber Brown, know that won't last. But I intend to enjoy it while it does.

I never thought in a million years, or a million dollars, that my great idea about Camp Sukkatukket would end up in a bunch of Amber and Fredrich jokes.

And I know my class. The jokes may have stopped for now, but they will definitely not be the last ones I hear.

Chapter
Eleven

I, Amber Brown, am Broadway bound.
Dad just picked me up for my big surprise
weekend. As we pull out of the driveway,
he says, "Part one of the surprise . . . . .
tonight I am taking you to see your first
Broadway musical."

I squeal. I can't help it. Normally I am
not a squealer, but Brenda, my Amber-
sitter, has been teaching me Broadway
songs ever since she and her boyfriend
were in their high school musical. I've
been teaching them to Brandi and Kelly.

That's one reason we're writing "Pickle Me Silly."

I sing Dad a sample lyric. Actually, it's our only lyric so far, but I love it:

> "Hey dilly dilly
> Pickle me silly . . .
> I go with pastrami
> Just don't tell my mommy."

Dad starts laughing. "That is the silliest song I ever heard," he says. "Why do I think it's so funny?"

"Because it is. Come on, sing it with me."

I teach Dad the lyrics and soon we are laughing so hard, we don't even mind getting stuck in the traffic at the Lincoln Tunnel.

We finally get out of the tunnel and drive uptown. "Okay, Amber, close your eyes," Dad says. "Part two is coming up. I don't want you to see it until we get there."

I squeeze my eyes tight, then open my right eye just a tiny bit.

I, Amber Brown, am not good at waiting for a surprise.

All I see are buildings.

Finally, Dad stops the car and sings out, "We're here! You can open your eyes now."

I open my eyes the rest of the way and look up.

We are in front of a huge stone building with a red carpet on the stairs. A man dressed in a red uniform with gold buttons opens the car door for me. I feel like a princess.

I step out. I am trying so hard not to squeal again.

"Welcome to the Plaza, Amber Brown."

"How does he know my name?" I whisper.

Dad is grinning from ear to ear. "I called ahead. This is your weekend to be Eloise. Remember when I used to read those books to you?"

Of course I remember. I start to quote the book to him.

"I am Eloise.
I am six.
I am a city child.
I live at the Plaza."

Mom and Dad read *Eloise* to me so many times when I was little, I almost knew it by heart. I always wanted to see the Plaza. Now I am not just going to see it, I am going to stay in it!

I put my arms around Dad and squeeze him tight.

Inside, things just get better and better. Another man in uniform takes our luggage and leads us to our room.

He opens the door. "Welcome to the Eloise Suite, Amber Brown."

Now I DO squeal. I'm starting to sound like a trained squeal.

I thought the room was called a "sweet" because it has candy-striped pink walls, just like the cover of the book. But it turns out that a "suite" in a hotel means you get more than one room. Dad's room is not pink.

My bed has the biggest, most princess-like headboard. It is pink with gold trim.

"Dad! This is amazing." I hop around my room like Eloise. "We are definitely in the pink!"

This is a phrase Aunt Pam taught me. It means everything is hunky-dory and you're feeling great.

"We really are, Amber. Or maybe I should say we're in the green. The company is so happy with my work that I just got a huge bonus. And I want to celebrate with the person I love most in the world, my little girl."

Dad looks so happy. I am happy too.

I also feel kind of funny. Mom and Max and I are being so careful about money right now. And here I am with Dad in a suite that must cost a small fortune.

As soon as we unpack, Dad says, "Part two of the surprise is the Eloise Suite. Part three . . . . . dinner on the town with your dad."

We go to a restaurant where he says lots of Broadway stars like to eat. We don't see any in person, but there are hundreds of signed pictures on the walls.

Dad orders me a "Shirley Temple." This is a drink made especially for kids . . . . my favorite part is the cherry.

After dessert Dad says, "Now, on to the show!"

He holds my hand tight while we walk.

I'm glad, because there are so many people it would be scary if he didn't.

When we go into the theater, I am amazed. The walls are painted gold and decorated from top to bottom with beautiful carvings.

"Can I decorate my room this way?" I ask.

Dad laughs. "I said I got a bonus, not that they gave me the company!"

Our seats are way up front.

The show is the best best best thing I have ever seen. It makes me laugh so hard, snot comes out my nose. I wonder if I am the first person to blow snot at a Broadway show. Luckily Dad passes me his handkerchief.

Ten minutes after that big laugh, I am crying. And I am not even sad. It's just that the stars are singing a song that is so beautiful it makes tears come out of my eyes. Maybe it's because the actors are right in front of me . . . . . live people telling me a story with songs and dance and music.

When the show ends, the whole audience stands up to cheer. I clap so hard my hands get sore.

After the show Dad holds my hand again as we half-walk, half-dance back to the Plaza.

When we get to our suite, I find a chocolate on my pillow. I, AMBER BROWN, WANT TO BE A BROADWAY STAR AND LIVE AT THE PLAZA!

The next morning, Dad tells me we

are going to take a carriage ride through Central Park before we go back to New Jersey. As we walk through the lobby, I spot a shop for girls. I guess it's there because of all the Eloise stuff.

In the window is a dress.

Not just any dress. THE dress.

The dress I have been looking for without even knowing what it looks like.

It is black and white—not pink. This dress has a black top with soft white ruffles around the neck. The bottom is white with lots of layers and little teardrops around the bottom. It's perfect.

Dad sees me staring at it.

"Amber?"

Now I am in a pickle and it's not silly. How do I tell Dad that I just found the dress I want to wear at Mom and Max's wedding?

"Amber, that dress would look great on you. Let's go in and you can try it on."

How can I say no?

We go into the shop. The saleslady gets the dress and leads me to a changing room. That's a good name for it because when I put the dress on, I, Amber Brown, feel different. It's as if it really has changed me.

I go out to show Dad.

He gets a huge smile on his face. "You look fabulous!" He turns to the saleslady. "We'll take it."

I am sooooooooo happy. I am also a little bit scared. What is Dad going to think when he finds out why I want the dress?

Dad and I haven't mentioned the wedding, or Mom and Max, once this weekend. We've been having such a great time. I don't want to ruin it.

Dad pays for the dress and we put it with our luggage in the lobby. It is now being guarded by another man in a uniform. I wonder if the Plaza has its own army. I wonder if they have privates and captains and generals. I wonder why I wonder things like this.

We go through the revolving door and down the red carpet. I'm getting used to that red carpet.

Across the street from the Plaza is a line of carriages. We go to the front of the line. The carriage driver is wearing a fancy black coat with tails and a black top hat. His horse is wearing a black top hat too, only his has holes for his ears to stick through. The horse is kind of droopy, but I like him anyway.

I pat the horse's nose. He shakes his head up and down.

"What's his name?" I ask.

"Max," the driver answers.

Dad bursts out laughing. "Perfect! We know another Max who's about to get hitched up."

I glare at him but don't say anything.

The driver holds my hand as he helps
me into the carriage. Dad hops up beside
me. The driver tucks a fuzzy blanket over
our legs. It's nice, but I am definitely not
feeling warm and fuzzy.

We clip-clop into Central Park. The
trees are still bare, but the park is full of
people running . . . . . walking . . . . .
bicycling. I am trying to enjoy it, but I'm

too angry with Dad for making that crack about Max.

I hear him chuckle again.

"What's so funny?" I snap.

"I love being pulled around by a horse named Max." He's leaning back with that smug look I hate.

I can't stand it.

"Dad, everything has been so perfect. Why do you always have to ruin it? I don't want you to make jokes about Max. Maybe you don't like that he and Mom are getting married, but they are. And I'm a big part of it. I hate that you and Mom got divorced. I didn't have any choice about that, but I have to live with what's happened. I'm trying hard and it's not easy. I like Max and I love you and I don't need you making this any harder for me than it already is!"

Dad's smile vanishes. He turns away and looks out at the park.

This makes me even madder.

"Dad, say something!"

He turns back, and his face is really, really sad. "I blew it," he says. "My counselor told me to make this weekend all about you and me, and not to talk about your mother and Max at all. And I was trying hard to do that. We've had such a wonderful weekend, and now I've messed up again. I'm sorry, Amber. I'm having a tough time with your mom getting remarried, and sometimes I say things I shouldn't."

Now it's my turn not to want to talk. I've been so wrapped up in Mom and Max's wedding, I guess I didn't want to think about how it made Dad feel.

Then there's what I just let him do at the dress shop. I know that I messed up too. I start to cry.

Dad puts his arm around me. He looks almost scared. "Amber, honey, what is it?

I know I upset you, but it's not that bad, is it?"

I shake my head. Then I take a deep breath. "We have to take the dress back."

"Why?"

"I wanted it so I could wear it at the wedding. But I was afraid you wouldn't buy it for me if I told you. That wasn't fair. It would be wrong for me to wear the dress that you got for me to Mom's wedding."

Dad squeezes my shoulder. "There's no need to take the dress back, honey."

"Why not?"

"I knew why you wanted it when I bought it for you."

"And you got it anyway?" I am amazed.

"I care a lot more about you than I do about that wedding. I want you to feel good while you're there. And I'm glad that you'll be wearing something that reminds you of me."

I snuggle next to Dad.

He squeezes me closer.

I sigh.

He sighs.

We hear what sounds like a giant sigh from somewhere ahead of us. Max, the horse, has lifted his tail.

I didn't realize that horses can poop and walk at the same time. It's quite a talent, even if they have to slow down to do it.

I can't help it. I start giggling. I look at Dad and I can see that he is biting his lips to hold in a laugh.

"It's okay." I pat his arm. "That was funny."

The laugh explodes out of him.

We settle back against the seat.

"I know I'm not a perfect dad, Amber. But I'm trying."

"You don't have to be perfect," I say. "Just be my dad."

Chapter Twelve

"Did you have fun?" Mom asks when I come through the door.

She almost looks like she hopes I will say no.

"I had a great time."

I feel like I should not sound too happy.

"What's in the shopping bag?"

I get a bad feeling. I thought she'd be excited that we could cross "Get Amber's Dress" off her list of things that have to be done. Now I'm not so sure.

"It's a dress. THE dress. The one I want to wear to the wedding."

Her mouth gets tight around the corners.

"Where did you get it?" She eyes the pink-and-gold box.

"Dad bought it for me at a shop at the Plaza. We were staying there."

"How much did it cost?"

I don't like her voice.

"I don't know. You taught me it isn't polite to ask how much a present costs."

"Well, if he bought it at the Plaza, it must have cost a bundle. Does he know you're planning to wear it to the wedding?"

I, Amber Brown, thought my dress problems were over . . . . now I know that I was wrong.

"Yes. He knows."

She shakes her head. "That's just like your father. He buys you a dress he knows

I can't afford. Mister Moneybags with his bonus and his red sports car and his take-my-daughter-to-the-Plaza weekends. He knows that if you wear that dress at the wedding, every time I look at you, I'll think of him. I don't want that, Amber. I don't want him to be part of this day. It's about the future, not the past."

"Well, maybe you don't want to have to look at me either," I shout. "I'm part of your past!"

I grab the bag and run up to my room. I slam my door.

I hear my mom on the stairs. "Amber!" she shouts.

"Don't come in!" I warn her. "I mean it!"

"Amber, we have to talk."

"Not now!"

I stand still for a second. I don't hear anything. I can't tell if she's still standing at the door or if she's gone to her own room. Right now I don't care. I'm just glad she's not coming in.

I pick up my gorilla. Dad won him for me at the town fair back when he and Mom were still together. I have had many long conversations with Gorilla, usually when I am upset. He is a very good listener . . . . . even if he never answers.

"It's getting worse."

Gorilla probably wonders what I mean.

"Now that Mom and Max are getting married, I thought she would stop getting so mad about Dad all the time. Every time it happens, I feel split in two. Now I can see that it will never stop, maybe not ever ever."

Gorilla just looks at me. Maybe if you're a gorilla who gets to hang out on my bed all day, you don't think about feeling split in two.

Mom knocks on my door again. "Amber, can we talk now?"

I get up and open the door. "Are you going to be nice?"

"I'll try."

I let her into my room. We both sit on the bed. The box with my dress in it is between us.

"I don't even know why we both got so

upset so fast." She smiles a little, but it's a kind of sad smile. "It's a funny thing about weddings, Amber. People tend to get a little crazy while they're planning them. Having a meltdown is almost part of the process."

"Why? It's supposed to be a happy day."

"That's part of the problem . . . . . you want everything to be so perfect. There are so many details to take care of and so many people to make happy and it all just gets too hard sometimes."

"I'm not 'people.' I'm me, Amber Brown. Your only child."

Mom sighs. "That's another part of the problem, a big one. It's not strangers we get mad at. It's the people closest to us."

"That's weird."

"We're a weird species. Haven't you noticed?"

"The last couple of weeks have made that pretty clear."

Mom glances at the box. "I'm sorry, Amber. I just don't want you wearing a dress that will remind me of him on my and Max's big day."

I get up and stand in front of her. "Mom, look at me."

She seems surprised.

I put my hands on her cheeks, pretending I am the mother and she is the kid. "Now you listen to me, Sarah Thompson."

I almost say "Sarah Brown," but I catch myself.

"I am your daughter. I'm also Dad's daughter. You said you don't want anything at the wedding to remind you of Dad. But what about me? When you look at me, you will be seeing part of him no matter what I'm wearing."

We both look at the dress box.

"Mom, Dad did NOT buy this dress to bug you. He bought it because I fell in love with it and because it looks great on me!"

She takes a deep breath. "All right." She reaches for the package. "Let me see it."

"No!" I say. "Don't open it. I want you to see it on me. Go downstairs and I'll come and model it for you."

Mom kisses me on the top of my head and leaves the room.

I take the dress out of the box . . . it's just as beautiful as I remembered. I put it on. At the top of the stairs I shout, "Cover your eyes!"

I walk down the stairs and stand in front of Mom. "Okay, you can look now."

Mom puts down her hands. Suddenly her eyes fill with tears.

"Please don't be unhappy about it. I love this dress. Don't you think it looks good on me?"

"Honey, it looks beautiful on you."

"Then why are you crying?"

"Because you look so grown up. Moms always cry a little bit about their children growing up."

Chapter Thirteen

Justin is here! Justin is here! Justin is here!

Well, not exactly here. But almost. Mr. Daniels just called to say that they're getting off the turnpike and are only a few minutes away.

I run outside and stand in the driveway so I will be three seconds closer.

Mom comes out and puts her hands on my shoulders. "I can't wait to hold that new baby! It seems like ages since we went down to visit last October."

I think about that and how much things

have changed since then. In October, Mom was still trying to decide whether to marry Max. That was why we went to Alabama . . . . . she wanted to talk to Mrs. Daniels about it in person.

Besides Aunt Pam, Justin's mom is the person my mother trusts the most.

Now the wedding is only a couple of days away. I'm finally going to see Justin again. The last time I saw him, he had gotten taller. Since then I've had a growth spurt too. I wonder what else might have changed while I wasn't looking?

Suddenly we hear a voice cry, "Yodel-hey-de-hoo!"

A green car turns into the drive-way . . . . . and keeps coming. I realize that's because it's hauling a camper-trailer behind it.

The instant the car stops, Justin leaps out from the backseat. "Amber!"

He runs toward me.

"Justin!"

I start toward him.

We stop. For a minute it seemed as if we were going to hug. That would be really weird . . . . . even though it's what the grown-ups are doing.

We stare at each other. I'm trying to see if Justin has changed. I can't spot anything . . . . at least nothing big. He hasn't grown a new ear or anything like that.

But his hair is longer, and he is so tan that I suddenly feel very pale.

"Yodel-hey-de-hoo," he calls, sounding like his father.

"What the heck is that supposed to be?"

"Yodeling!" Justin says proudly. "Dad taught me and Danny how to yodel on the way up."

"One thousand miles." Mrs. Daniels sighs. "One thousand long, ear-battering miles. But believe it or not, baby Paula seems to think it's a lullaby. So does Danny. They're both sleeping right now."

"I want to see her!" Mom exclaims.

Mrs. Daniels goes to the car and comes back holding baby Paula.

"I want to see her too!" I cry, squeezing between Mom and Justin.

Justin makes a face. "Everyone makes such a fuss over babies." But he can't keep from smiling.

I can tell that he's going to be a really good big brother to her.

Mrs. Daniels hands the baby to Mom. Mom cradles baby Paula in her arms. She smiles at me. It is one of the happiest smiles I have ever seen. Suddenly I realize that in a year or two, I might be a big sister.

The idea is a little scary. Before I can think about it too much, Mr. Daniels calls for me and Justin to help him unpack.

We unpack and unpack and unpack. I look at the pile of stuff on the driveway. "I can't believe how much you guys crammed into this car."

"And you haven't even seen what's in the camper yet," Justin says.

Mr. Daniels laughs. "I think my great-great-grandfather had less stuff in his covered wagon when he crossed the prairie than we needed for one baby, one four-year-old, and what Justin's mom wanted to bring for the wedding." He pulls out a little suitcase. "Justin's and my stuff is all in here."

We get everything into the house, including Danny, who looks groggy and sticky.

"Want to visit our chewing gum ball?" I ask Justin.

"Is it much bigger?"

"The bigger it gets, the slower it grows. I think it misses you. I don't chew gum so much now that you're not here."

"Neither do I," Justin says. He smacks his forehead. "Oh, no! Does that mean we're growing up?"

I laugh. We go upstairs to my room. The ball is in my closet. It is still in the box Justin used when he gave me custody. We both look at it.

Justin picks it up. "It's smaller than I remember."

"You were smaller the last time you saw it."

Justin smiles. "Do you have any gum?"

"I was hoping you would ask! I've been saving some special for when you got here."

I go to my desk drawer and take out the gum.

Adding new gum to the ball is tricky. You can't add it too soon or it's too juicy, so you have to chew it for a while first.

When we are ready, we carefully stretch the fresh pieces over the ball of old gum. They are bright and slick.

Justin stands back to examine our work. He smiles. "That looks better."

Just then we hear the front door open.

"Max and Aunt Pam are here!" I shout.

We run downstairs. Mom is introducing Max to Mr. and Mrs. Daniels. Aunt Pam hugs me. Mrs. Daniels hugs Max. Mr. Daniels hugs Aunt Pam. It's a little hug festival.

Max holds out his hand. "And you must be Justin. Amber has told me so much about you."

Justin looks a little shy as he shakes Max's hand, but I can tell he's relieved that he's not getting hugged.

Watching them makes me remember when I didn't know Max. I wouldn't even say his name . . . I kept calling him

"What's-His-Face." Now Max is a big part of my life, and a really good one.

"Okay, we're all here, let's order the pizza." Mom goes to the phone.

"Amber's favorite food group." Max grins. "Yours too, Justin?"

"Totally, as long as you remember to . . . . ." He looks at me, and we say it together. "Hold the anchovies!"

We hold up our fingers, pretending to be the pizza guy holding the wiggly anchovies.

Mrs. Daniels laughs. "You two will never change."

I think about that later, when I am in my room, trying to go to sleep.

It's not really true. Even though I sometimes wish they wouldn't, things are changing. Justin and me . . . . Mom and Max . . . . everything. It all keeps changing.

The grown-ups are still downstairs in

the kitchen. Every once in a while I hear them laughing.

Tonight the house is filled with people I love. But it is the last night that will happen. In two days Mom and Max will be married. When they come back from their honeymoon, we will be moving. So this is the last time that the house I grew up in will ever be filled this way again.

I can't help it. I cry a little.

Chapter
Fourteen

I hand Justin a big box. It's filled with glue and birdseed and glitter and rolls of ribbon and netting.

"What's this stuff for?"

"You'll see. It's a surprise for the bride and groom. Take it out to Max's car."

I carry my dress. It's on a hanger and covered by a garment bag.

I give Justin the front seat, partly because I want to ride in the back to protect my dress . . . . . . partly because I want to give Max and Justin a chance to get to know each other.

Aunt Pam leads the way. She honks as she heads out with Mom.

Mr. Daniels sticks his head out of the car and yodels.

Justin rolls down his window and yodels back.

"We're like a caravan," I say to Justin. "Well, except for the yodeling. The only thing missing is the camels. Remember when Mr. Cohen turned our classroom into a caravan to Egypt?"

"That was one of my favorites."

Back in third grade, when Justin and I were still in the same class, we loved our teacher. He had us make passports, and we took "trips" to countries all around the world. We got a stamp for every country we visited.

We explain all this to Max. "Well, this caravan is going to Camp Sukkatukket," he says.

Justin sticks his head between the seats so he can see me. "Maybe they should call it Camp Boogertukket," he whispers.

I know he thinks I will laugh at this. And I kind of feel like I should. But I even more feel like I shouldn't.

Justin looks puzzled and turns so he is facing forward again.

We get out into the country. Max says, "You should have been with us the first time Amber brought us out here, Justin. Everything was a mix of snow and mud."

"We almost never get snow in Alabama. I miss it. My dad says that's because I don't have to drive in it."

I look out the window. The cherry trees are covered with pink and white blossoms. The willow trees have turned that light green I love. Bright yellow patches of daffodils decorate many yards. I realize that I like living in a place with four seasons.

When we pull into the narrow road that leads to Camp Sukkatukket, Max shouts, "Look!"

He stops the car.

Beside the road is a sign that says

Welcome to
Sarah and Max's
Wedding

"This makes it so real," Max says. "Wait a second while I get a picture." He bounds out of the car.

"I bet Fredrich and his father made the sign," I tell Justin.

"Do you think we should check it for Fredrich's boogers?"

Max gets back into the car before I can say anything. That's probably good, because I'm starting to get a little angry about Justin's jokes.

When we pull into the camp, the others are already there.

Fredrich and his father are standing with them.

Mom runs to Max and hugs him. "Did

you see our sign? Wasn't it sweet? Mr.
Allen was just telling us that he and Fredrich made it."

Justin pokes me in the ribs. I am about
to tell him to cut out the booger jokes
when Fredrich shouts, "Hey, Justin! I
didn't know you were going to be here!"

Before I know it, Fredrich is taking
Justin and Danny down to the waterfront
to show them the boats.

Nobody even thinks to ask me.

I suddenly remember they're boys. At
least they're being friendly. I'm glad they
like each other. They just can't like each
other more than they like me.

Chapter
Fifteen

I, Amber Brown, have glittery fingers.

I also have birdseedy fingers.

These party favors are a lot harder to make than I thought they would be.

I am glad Brandi and Kelly got here. They are really good at crafts.

I like doing crafts, and I love glitter. But I have so many things on my mind right now . . . . . especially the toast that I still haven't written . . . . that I keep messing things up.

Justin, Fredrich, and Danny are not helping. In fact, they are un-helping. A few minutes ago they had a small birdseed war. I now have birdseed in my hair and in my lap as well as glued to my fingers. The only ones who are really happy are the sparrows who just got a free meal.

"The birdseed is to throw at the bride and groom AFTER the wedding, not at each other right now," Brandi says sternly.

The boys settle down and we get an assembly line going.

Brandi and Kelly make tags that say SARAH AND MAX in glittery letters. They let Danny help sprinkle the glitter.

Fredrich is putting birdseed in squares of netting.

I have the wrap-up job . . . which really is wrapping up. When Fredrich slides a packet of netting and seed to me, I tie it up with a piece of ribbon. Then I pass it to Justin, who ties the other end of the ribbon to one of the glittery tags.

Once we all get going, it's a lot of fun. I love working with my friends this way.

When I think this, I am surprised to realize that I consider Fredrich one of my friends. When did that happen?

"Finished!" Justin says when he ties on the last tag.

We call Aunt Pam to come look.

"Very nice. Your mom is going to love these."

I feel good. The bags of birdseed look beautiful in the bright netting.

"What's next?" Brandi asks. She's

counted the favors twice to make sure we have enough.

"I have to practice my toast."

I don't mention that I haven't written it yet.

"Great!" Kelly says. "Practice on us."

I shake my head and mumble, "I'm not ready."

Justin is looking at me.

"Just try it," Brandi insists. "It doesn't have to be perfect."

"No, I want it to be a surprise."

"Do you want to see the camp?" Fredrich asks.

"Sure," Brandi and Kelly say together.

Danny runs down the porch steps. "I want to see the boats again!"

"Will you guys watch Danny?" Justin asks. "I'll stay here. I have something I need to work on too."

"Sure," Kelly says. "He's cute."

Justin rolls his eyes.

When the others have gone, I ask Justin what he needs to work on.

"Helping you."

"Helping me do what?"

"Your toast. You haven't written it yet, have you?"

"How did you know?"

He smiles. "We've been friends since preschool, Amber. You always put things off . . . . . especially when they're important. Come on, let's get to work."

"What do you know about giving a toast?" I ask.

"Nothing. But we'll figure it out. What are best friends for?"

Chapter Sixteen

The ceremony is about to start. Mom and Max and I are on the side porch, ready to make our entrance. Rose and Herman are at the front of the Grand Salon, surrounded by their instruments. Their music sounds even more beautiful than the night we heard it at their house.

I walk in first, then turn to watch Mom and Max. When we are all at the front of the room, Rose and Herman put down their instruments. Rose comes to stand in front of us.

Mom hands me her flowers and gives me a kiss. Then she takes Max's hands.

Rose turns to the guests. "Sarah and Max have written their own vows."

She nods at Mom.

Mom clears her throat and says, "I, Sarah, take you, Max, to be my husband, through up, through down, through good and bad, through things that change and things that stay the same."

I start to cry. Mom told me she and Max were writing their own vows, but I hadn't heard them until now.

Max repeats the words to Mom, except he says "I, Max" instead of "I, Sarah."

When he is done, Rose smiles and says, "I now pronounce you husband and wife."

Mom and Max kiss . . . . . it's a humdinger. They look like they should be in a movie.

That's when it hits me. Mom and Max are married.

Even so, I hope they're not going to be kissing like this around the house all the time.

That would be gross.

Chapter Seventeen

I am looking out at the tables. So many friends. So many relatives.

Before, I was terrified to do this, but with Justin's help I have my toast ready.

The biggest problem was that my dress didn't have any pockets to hold the paper I wrote it on. So Justin sneaked it under my plate.

Everyone loves the dumplings. Everyone is talking and laughing. Someone starts tapping a spoon against a glass. Soon everyone is tapping. The room is filled with a kind of ringing sound.

Aunt Pam leans over to me. "That's a signal that they want the bride and groom to kiss."

"Again?"

Max leans over and kisses Mom.

Everyone cheers and claps.

Some things about weddings are very strange.

A minute later, Max leans over and touches my shoulder.

It's time.

I swallow hard and stand up. Everyone is talking and laughing, and at first they don't notice me. Then someone at the closest table starts saying, "Shhh, shhh!"

The shushing spreads. Soon the room is quiet.

I look out at them. My heart is pounding, but it is also filled with happiness.

I raise my glass. It is filled with sparkling cider.

The grown-ups have champagne.

"I would like to propose a toast."

Everyone is listening carefully now.

I unfold my paper and read.

"I will admit that when I first met Max, I didn't like the idea of him going out with my mom. In fact, I was a little bratty about it."

People nod and smile. Max blushes a little.

"Now I am so happy that they did. I did not want my life to change. But no matter what I do, it keeps happening. Some of the changes are bad. Some are very very good.

"This is one of the best changes ever."

I don't need to read the next part. I look right at Mom and Max.

"We had some problems on the way
But we've survived. It's your big day.
Here's the truth, I'm not pretending
It's a fairy tale with a happy ending.

So here's to Mom and here's to Max—
I love you both and them's the facts.
Now that you're married,
what do I think?
I, Amber Brown, am tickled pink!"

A word from the real Amber Brown

"Aunt," my seven-year-old self said to Paula Danziger, in my deep truck-driver voice, "why don't you write a book for younger kids?" At the time, Paula was only writing novels for young adults. This badgering occurred often and went on for several years.

Then one day:

"Aunt," I sobbed into the phone, "I'm losing my two best friends. Ben and Dylan are both moving away." Without my friends, the new school year looked miserable. Paula calmed me down and was very supportive, as she always was. Paula had the biggest heart of anyone I have ever known and was always there when I (or anyone else) needed her.

I am the real-life Amber Brown. I am also Paula's only niece, Carrie Danziger.

Paula took my nagging for a book for younger readers and the tragedy of my best friends moving away plus many of her own experiences and ideas to give birth to Amber Brown.

By the time *Amber Brown Is Not a Crayon* was published, I was already reading Paula's older works, such as *The Cat Ate My Gymsuit,* but the Amber Brown series exceeded all of my expectations—it became Paula's masterpiece and a major part of her legacy.

Even though the world is very different today than it was when she began writing in the 1970s, the troubles and the turmoil of her characters remain the same as today's young readers. Paula strove to relate to people on a personal level through her work and was successful because she was such a "people person."

Paula had so much love to give that she needed many recipients. She had many "best" friends in her life. Two of these friends, Elizabeth Levy and Bruce Coville, are pertinent to the novel that you just read. They still jokingly refer to each other as "Paula's best friend" and "Paula's other best friend."

Bruce and Paula had been friends since the time of the dinosaurs. Long, long, LONG ago, they began reading and critiquing each other's work over the phone. They re-created this process several times at conferences, sitting back to back as if they were on the phone.

Bruce knew Paula and Paula's writing very well. He is the author of many science fiction adventures, including the My Teacher Is an Alien series. Even though their genres are very different, Bruce and Paula were able to edit and support each other as writers.

Liz and Paula were friends for a long time but not quite

as long as Bruce and Paula. Liz is the author of the Fletcher mystery series and MANY other books. Liz and Paula used to run into each other at writing events around the country. They always meant to get together when they were back in New York, but somehow never did. Finally, after years of running into each other on the road, Paula said to Liz, "Either we're going to do this, or we're not!" From that point on they were best friends; they would speak on the phone every day and frequently traveled up and down the west side of Manhattan to see each other.

Almost all of Paula's friends heard at one time or another, "You're going to love this person, but you can't love them more than you love me." Paula loved to network her friends together, and she is the reason that Bruce, Liz and I are friends.

Paula's close connection with Bruce, Liz and my family is the reason why they were asked to co-write *Amber Brown Is Tickled Pink*. Paula always intended there to be more Amber Brown books and this was lovingly written to preserve her legacy as well as Amber's.

As Paula always said, "Amber Brown would not be complete without the illustrations." Thank you to Tony Ross for illustrating the Amber Brown books for all of these years and continuing to bring her to life in the latest rendition. *Amber Brown Is Tickled Pink* also needed and received the support of the people at Writers House and Putnam. Thank you to everyone involved for allowing the world to continue to hear Paula's voice. Thank you to all of Paula's readers and fans who keep Amber and all of Paula's other characters not only alive but close to their hearts.

Thank-yous would not be complete without a thank-you to Paula, who not only shaped my life but continues to shape the lives of her readers through her books.

—Carrie Danziger